CHRISTMAS IN

MY SOUL

CHRISTMAS IN MY SOUL

A Second Collection

Compiled and Edited by

JOE WHEELER

Doubleday

New York London Toronto Sydney Auckland

PUBLISHED BY DOUBLEDAY
a division of Random House, Inc.
1540 Broadway, New York, NY 10036

DOUBLEDAY and the portrayal of an anchor with a
dolphin are registered trademarks of Doubleday,
a division of Random House, Inc.

Book design by Dana Leigh Treglia

Woodcut illustrations from the library of Joe Wheeler

Library of Congress Cataloging-in-Publication Data

Christmas in my soul: a second collection / edited and
with an introduction by Joe Wheeler.
p. cm.
Contents: Red shoes / Anita L. Fordyce—Small things /
Margaret E. Sangster, Jr.—The miraculous staircase /
Arthur Gordon—Christmas magic / Christine Whiting
Parmenter—The man who missed Christmas / J. Edgar
Parks—Grr-face / Gary B. Swanson.
1. Christmas stories, American.
I. Wheeler, Joe L., 1936–
PS648.C45 C448 2001
813'.0108334—dc21
00-065871

ISBN 0-385-49860-8
Copyright © 2001 by Joe Wheeler

1 3 5 7 9 10 8 6 4 2

She was the spark that lit the Christmas flame in me.
The voice that first told the Christmas stories that are
now such a part of me. It thus gives me great joy
to dedicate the first two *Christmas in My Soul*
collections to my beloved mother
—mentor, teacher, inspiration, and friend—

BARBARA LEININGER WHEELER

Acknowledgments

Introduction: "We Get Letters—Lots and Lots of Letters," by Joe Wheeler. Copyright © 1996 (revised 2000). Printed by permission of the author.

"Red Shoes," by Anita L. Fordyce. Copyright © 1983. Reprinted by permission of the author.

"Small Things," by Margaret E. Sangster, Jr. Published in Sangster's *The Littlest Orphan and Other Christmas Stories*, Round Table Press, New York, 1928. If anyone can provide knowledge of origin and first publication source of this old story, please relay this information to Joe Wheeler, care of Doubleday Religion Department.

"The Miraculous Staircase," by Arthur Gordon. Published in *Guideposts Magazine*, May 1956, and in

Contents

CHRISTMAS IN MY SOUL

INTRODUCTION

....

We Get Letters—
Lots and Lots of Letters

Joseph Leininger Wheeler

We get letters . . ." I remember that line from the old *Perry Como Show* (how *that* dates me!). Back then I thought, *Wouldn't it be exciting to get lots and lots of letters?* These days, almost every mail brings letters—lots and lots of letters. And like that wonderfully wacky *I Love Lucy* episode where the assembly line belt speeds up faster and faster, well, that's the way with my letters. And I'm no more able to keep up with them than Lucy was able to keep up with the chocolates on her runaway conveyor belt.

I get letters responding to stories, suggesting stories, and with stories. And each new story collection that is published launches another wave of letters. But does all this mean I don't want any more? Not on your life! Letters are the very lifeblood of these continuing anthologies.

HOW STORIES ARE CHOSEN

In letters and on talk shows, one of the most frequently asked questions is this one: "How do you choose which stories appear in a given collection?"

Well, it's this way. Let's say that you read one of my introductions and note my plea for more stories. Not just *any* stories, but the ones that move you deeply. So you decide to search your personal story files to see if there are any that stand out from the rest—the ones you just can't seem to get out of your head. You know, like that haunting melody that keeps sweeping the harp strings of your soul, and doesn't ever leave . . . so you couldn't forget it if you tried.

As you search through the story treasures of the years, suddenly you stop. *Ah, here it is! I'd wondered where this old story was! Been years since I last read it, but when I was young I'd have it read to me over and over and over again!*

So you make a copy of the cherished old story, write me a covering letter, then mail it to me, care of my publisher. When I receive it, I scan it, then place it in a stack of story submissions, there to wait until I have an oasis of time where I can stop everything else, wall out the world, and step into the never-never land of stories.

First of all, I search my files to see whether or not I already have the story. If I don't, I make up a folder for it, then write on the front your name and the date you submitted it. If I already have it, I add your name to any others who may have submitted it before. Each submission counts as a vote. The more votes it receives, the more serious I take the story.

Each submission moves the story up a notch in my story collection. As time passes, and submissions continue, certain stories, like cream, rise to the top. All such stories are considered future anthology finalists and are reread each time the selection process begins for a new collection.

But it doesn't always work that way: Sometimes I am so deeply moved by my first reading of a story that I just sit there at the end, limp with emotional exhaustion, and my eyes filled with tears. After finishing, I write my gut feeling code on the folder (with five stars being the highest rating and one star the lowest).

My wife Connie is usually my first victim. If a given story moves *her*—since it takes more to bring her to tears than it does me—then I know I have a certified winner! If it passes *that* test, then I unleash it on relatives and friends who stray within range, and I keep tabs on their responses. If the story makes it through that gamut, it is propelled in one quantum jump from the bottom tier to the top tier of the collection.

HOW I GOT INTERESTED IN STORIES

It's amazing how often I am asked this question. I tell those who write, as well as interviewers, that I am convinced beyond a shadow of a doubt that God preordained me for this ministry of stories—in that respect, I feel a kinship to Cyrus in Holy Writ who God preordained for a specific role. God had me born into a very special home, with a father who was an educator, a minister, and a missionary; and with a mother who was—and still remains today—an elocutionist of the old school. Mother memorized hundreds and hundreds of poems, readings, and stories; some of the poems as long as Longfellow's *Evangeline* and *Hiawatha!*

During those crucial growing-up years, I was home-schooled in Latin America by this remarkable woman. Whenever I replay (from the archives of my memory) a videotape of those years, I see and hear again my mother reading and reciting. Her voice is even today an essential part of who I am. When Mother tells a story, it is virtual reality. Her diction is flawless, and she never knowingly mispronounces or misenunciates a word. She plays words like Fritz Kreisler played his Stradivarius: with all the emotions assaulted as her voice sobs, sighs, sings, and soars. She does not merely read a story, she does not merely tell a story—she *lives* a story! Once she gets into a given story, her audience is willy-nilly forced into that world and does not reenter their other world until she decides to set it free when her story is told.

So it was that through my mother—and through her father, Herbert Norton Leininger, a grand figure of a man who tread the boards of his Arcata, California, home with Shakespeare and Kipling—I gained my love of both the spoken and the written word. I grew up a voracious reader and devoured libraries wherever I went.

Returning to America, I majored first in religion, then moved on to English and history, earning master's degrees in the latter two, before going on to Vanderbilt University for my Ph.D. in English (with a history of ideas emphasis).

And during thirty-four years of teaching, I kept devouring books and stories—and collecting them. I found that I was a prisoner of my past: Like it or not, I had inherited my mother's obsession with Judeo-Christian, tear-jerky stories—you know, the ones that leave you limp and tear-stained at the end.

My students, I discovered, loved stories too. In fact, years afterward, some would write me, telling me how much these stories meant to them, how they would wake up in the middle of the night *hearing* my voice reading stories. I have since concluded that few greater bonds can we humans create than those forged by reading out loud.

HOW THESE STORY ANTHOLOGIES HAPPENED

It all started with a simple question asked by a coed at Columbia Union College in November of 1989: "Dr. Wheeler, have you ever thought of writing a Christmas story?" Two years later, then acquisitions editor at Review and Herald Publishing Association Penny Estes Wheeler asked me, "Joe, what have you been writing lately?" I answered,

"Oh, a couple of Christmas stories."

"Is that all?"

"Yes, but I've been collecting them all my life."

"What kind?"

"Well, the kind that you can't read without crying—and the ones that are Christ–centered rather than Santa Claus–centered."

She answered, "You know, there's a real vacuum in the market for that kind of a collection. Why don't you put together such an anthology, and send it to me?"

Sometime later, after I had submitted the collection, she phoned me and said, "Joe, the committee has cried its way through your manuscript. May we publish it?"

And thus was born *Christmas in My Heart* in 1992. There was no number on it, for none of us ever expected there to be another. But since it went through two printings before Christmas, my editor asked me to put together another. By the third collection, Dr. James Dobson had fallen in love with the stories, and sent out copies of "The Tiny Foot" all over the world. Two years later, Dr. Mark Fretz, then senior religion editor at Doubleday, suggested taking the series into the secular market, observing, "Joe, why would you limit this wonderful series to just Christian bookstore buyers? Let's take them *everywhere*." And thus was born the Doubleday hardback *Christmas in My Heart* series. Focus on the Family and Tyndale began publishing their own edition in 1998. As the millennium turned, Doubleday decided to rename its series *Christmas in My Soul*.

But readers wanted more than just Christmas stories, hence Focus on the Family launched the *Great Stories Remembered* series in 1996, and the *Great Stories Classic Books* in 1997; the Tyndale/Focus on the Family *Heart to*

Heart stories began in 1998; and WaterBrook/Random House launched the *Stories of Life* series in 1999.

Looking back, it's hard to believe that all this could happen so quickly: God moving me out of the formal classroom so that my wife Connie and I could devote the rest of our lives to the preservation of the old-timey value-based story. I draw most heavily from a period I call "The Golden Age of Judeo Christian Stories: 1870s–1950s."

HOW MY OWN STORIES EVOLVE

Unknowingly, I started something in the first *Christmas in My Heart* book by including two of my own stories, "The Snow of Christmas" and "Meditation in a Minor Key." Since that time almost every one of my collections has included one of my own stories (usually at the end); I also write an introduction to each collection and an introduction to each story in the book.

Over time, I have become more and more convinced that the best stories are cowritten by God. As each manuscript deadline nears, I ask God to sweep Joe Wheeler aside, and fill me with Him—to give me the plot. He has, and does. Almost invariably I run into dead-end streets during the writing, and am forced to ask God for further directions. Always, He sends me a celestial fax, and the story is able to continue.

For no story God and I ever cowrote have I ever received more mail than "Meditation" in Doubleday's *Christmas in My Heart—3.* Of its impact, a cherished friend, Louise Watson of South Carolina, wrote, "Didn't put it down until I had read every word, as I found every sentence fascinating. It was not only unique and delightful, but was something far more—it was food for the soul. As I finished each page I passed it on to Stan, who was seated in the lounge chair close by, and when we both finished reading it several hours later we looked at each other speechless and both of us had eyes filled with tears. What a powerful story!"

Another dear friend, Virginia Fagal from California, wrote of it, "Your story . . . is a real *treasure*. I stretched out on my couch one Friday night and read it through in one sitting. I marveled at your intimate knowledge of how musicians think and feel, as well as how music is constructed. *Such convincing detail*, I thought over and over. I don't know if you realize that my instrument is the violin, my major in college, and before arthritis stiffened some of my fingers, I played 'Meditation' scores of times. It, and the Mendelssohn *Violin Concerto*, were, in my opinion, divinely inspired. In using your consummate skills with words and ideas to bring forth a story of this magnitude and power for good, it was God and Joe Wheeler all the way."

Letters like these make all the sweat, blood, and tears that go into writing such a story well worth the price paid.

For readers of this book, an explanation is in order. For every *Christmas in My Heart* book (the longest-running Christmas series), I reduce hundreds of stories down to an average of fifteen to nineteen, thus what's left is pure gold; for the *Christmas in My Soul* gift books, we reduce those by another two-thirds, leaving only the platinum, *la crème de la crème*. Since we are left with an average of six stories, I do not include any of my own, as they tend to be quite long.

WOULD YOU READ
MY STORY?

Also part of the mail flow are stories written by the writers of the letters; or, a bit less often, stories submitted on behalf of another. Some of those who submit stories are professional writers, some are amateur writers, and some are daring to submit their brainchildren for the very first time.

Maimu Veedler of Ontario, Canada, submitted a story written by a local freelance writer, Cathy Miller. We included "Delayed Delivery" in *Christmas in My Heart—2* and in Doubleday's fourth collection. Thanks to those two inclusions and to Dr. James Dobson of Focus on the Family, that story went all over the world.

On a dare, an Alberta housewife who had *never* shared a story with anyone outside her immediate family sent in her true heartfelt story, "Charlie's Blanket." Thanks to its inclusion in *Christmas in My Heart—4*, as well as the first Doubleday collection, and its being chosen as the Focus on the Family Christmas story of the year, it too has now been read and heard by millions of people. . . . So one never knows what may happen to a given story.

YOU FOUND MY
LONG-LOST STORY!

Many letters have to do with the writer's excitement of discovering a story heard many years before, a story the writer had searched in vain for all through the intervening years, and now, lo and behold, here it is!

No other long-lost stories have elicited a more heartfelt response than "A Few Bars in the Key of G" [Doubleday *Christmas in My Heart—2* collection], "Candle in the Forest" [Doubleday *Christmas in My Heart—2* collection], "The Littlest Orphan" [Doubleday *Christmas in My Heart—3* collection], "Why the Minister Did Not Resign" [Doubleday *Christmas in My Soul—1*], and "Christmas in Tin Can Valley" [Doubleday *Christmas in My Soul—1*].

Typical of such responses are these lines from Linda Steinke of Alberta, who has since then become a cherished friend: "I was in bookworm's heaven devouring each story over the holidays. But the juiciest morsel was finding a story that my college dean of women read to us Christmas story lovers over twenty years ago. You can't imagine how I've searched for the story 'A Few Bars in the Key of G.' No available Christmas storybook was left unscanned. Alas, to no avail! What a delightful treat it was to find it in your book."

YOU MADE DAD CRY

Many letters deal with the emotional impact the stories have, both on those who read them and those who are read *to*. Especially are *men* a frequently mentioned subject. Macho men who are supposedly impervious to emotion apparently come unglued when they try to read one of these Christmas stories out loud.

When questioned about why my stories are different in this respect, I tell them that unless a given story moves me deeply it will never make it into one of my collections (hence people measure my stories by how many Kleenex it takes to get a reader through a given story). I also tell them that most Christmas collections that I've read down through the years are so sterile and emotionless that they left me dry-eyed. I determined that if I ever had the opportunity to put my own collections together, no story would be included that did not shake me to the core of my being. No matter how famous the author, there would be no exceptions to this basic rule of selection.

And the values are crucial as well. Stories which fail to incorporate in some way the reason we celebrate Christmas have no place in the series. It is this crucial principle which people tell me separates these collections from so many others. In truth, unless a story brings a Higher Power in, the story will lack the power to move one deeply, to change one's behavior for the better, to make the reader kinder, more loving, and committed to a life of service.

BLACK-BELTED
STORY COLLECTORS

As I look back over the last ten years, I want to publicly thank those who have done so much to make these story collections possible. Here and there throughout the United States and Canada are those who have earned the right to wear a "black belt" in story collecting. They are *serious*, lifelong collectors of stories. Most have been gathering such collections for many years and are very sophisticated where stories are concerned.

Many send letters and packets that include a rather uneven level of stories—some may be powerful, some so-so, and others may lack any power at all. Such submissions are typical, but most appreciated, for out of such packets have come some real winners.

But there are others who have such story sensitivity and expertise that every story has the potential of being a home run. Whenever I see a packet from one of these connoisseurs of great stories in my mail, my heart speeds up, for I know, even before I open the package, that I am in for a treat!

Some of the most moving stories have come from Dottie Davidson (Michigan) and her daughter-in-law Virginia Davidson (Washington). Another such intergenerational collaboration is that of Bessie Ellison (Washington) and her granddaughter, Corrie Whitney (California). These women really *know* stories!

Then there is Laura Drown of Massachusetts, who sent me her treasured scrapbook, the fruit of a lifetime of collecting! Patti Hare (Maryland) entrusted to us the personal story collection of her late father-in-law, the legendary storyteller Eric B. Hare, so that we could make copies of the stories we didn't have. Genevieve Gyes (Washington) often brightens my day with her letters and serendipitous submissions. Mildred McConnell

(California) has been one of the most faithful submitters. One of the sharpest story scouts I have ever known is Kay Prins (California). Almost every story she has ever sent me is good enough to make it into one of my anthologies. What an acquisitions editor she would make! Marilyn Nelson (Washington) is perhaps my most faithful and indefatigable story-submitter. So organized is she that she structures her submissions thematically, complete with observations and story origins. She can smell a winner a mile off!

Teresa Sales (Colorado) loaned me her lifetime collection of stories, as did Valeetah Motscheidler (Maryland), who let us photocopy her collection of over 1,400 pages; Barbara Reinholtz (Michigan) let us photocopy her collection of over 1,000 pages; and Lorena Widstrand (Utah) hand-delivered her vast collection for us to study.

I've become convinced over the years that deans of women are the greatest users of good stories of all. Longtime dean Beth Lowry (Texas) lent us her collection of a lifetime; and Lois Berry and Kathy Oliver (California) sent us the collection of that famous dean, the late Evabelle Winning (and incidentally, my cousin).

To story aficionados like these, nothing is treasured more than their heirloom stories. While we are working with them, we treat such collections like the fragile museum pieces they are.

There are hundreds and hundreds of others who have sent in stories and thus helped us to expand the collection to its present state. Each of them has blessed our lives and extended our circle of friendships in a very special way.

ABOUT THIS COLLECTION

While this is the second yearly *Christmas in My Soul* collection, it is the sixth annual collection by Doubleday, the first four being titled *Christmas in My Heart*. Thus new readers will wish to pick up copies of the earlier collections. Of the six authors presented in this collection, our readers will already be familiar with Christine Whiting Parmenter ("David's Star of Bethlehem") in the second treasury; and Margaret E. Sangster, Jr. ("The Lonely Tree," "The Littlest Orphan and the Christ Baby," and "With a Star on Top") in the second and third *Christmas in My Heart* and first *Christmas in My Soul* treasuries.

CODA

Virtually every day's mail brings welcome correspondence from you. Many of your letters are testimonials to the power of certain stories; virtually *all* of them express gratitude for the series. Others include favorite stories for possible inclusion down the line (some of them Christmas-related and others tying in with other genre collections we are working on). These letters from you not only brighten each day for us, but help to provide the stories that make possible future story anthologies.

May the good Lord bless and guide each of you.

You may contact me at the following address:

Joe L. Wheeler, Ph.D.

c/o Doubleday Religion Department

1540 Broadway

New York, New York 10036

RED SHOES

Anita L. Fordyce

In almost every day's mail, we get stories: stories that are merely stories, stories that are a cut above average, stories that are memorable enough to include in one of our collections, and stories that put us out of commission—as is the case with this story. After picking up our mail on our way out of town on a trip, Connie opened the packet, pulled out this true story, was intrigued by the title, and began reading it out loud.

We almost had to stop the car!

hristmas Eve day dawned, a Currier and Ives sort of day, with a wet, soft snow. Normally, snow, especially for Christmas, lightened my spirits; but not today. All night long I had continually rehearsed my five-year-old daughter, Jeney's, questions.

"Why did God give me crippled feet? Special shoes don't make them any better. Why can't I wear shoes like other girls wear?"

I had no answers, only the belief that God doesn't make mistakes. But she couldn't understand. Jeney had a condition called hypermobile feet, aggravated by poorly developed leg muscles and rheumatoid arthritis. More than flat, they turned over at the ankles. Her doctor said there was a possible corrective surgery, but for now orthopedic shoes would be best. The surgery, he cautioned, would permanently fuse her feet and give her stiff ankles for the rest of her life.

"I hate the shoes!" she cried. "They are ugly and always brown-brown, like boys wear."

They were always bulky, too, in order to accommodate an orthotic—a special ankle brace. In early December her doctor had given her a new shoe prescription. We usually ordered them from a shoe store, but this time we had been recommended to a semiretired shoemaker in our little New England village. He hand stitched specialty shoes for only a select few customers, so getting him to consider us hadn't been easy.

At a prearranged time we entered his dusty workshop that doubled as an antique shop. The only thing to remind us of the coming holiday was a large sleigh bell that jingled when the door shut behind us. The shoemaker, a large man with silver hair, was sitting at an oversized sewing machine in the back of a cluttered shop. He acknowledged our entrance with a cursory look over the top of half glasses that looked like the spectacles one pictured Santa Claus wearing. It was obvious we were to wait.

Finally, he laid down his work and slowly rose, steadying his balance upon the arm of the sewing machine. We were shocked to see him hobble toward us. Our eyes automatically dropped to his large, obviously deformed feet shrouded in odd-shaped black shoes. He stood in front of us only a few seconds. Out of breath, he sat down on the edge of a large flat table and looked down at my high-heeled shoes.

"You'll ruin your feet," he said in a raspy voice.

"We're here to talk about new shoes for Jeney," I said, gathering my courage. Intimidated, Jeney had ducked around my back. I took her hand and drew her out to face the tired man. "Her doctor has given us a new shoe prescription, and we're told you make the best."

"It's the holidays, you know." He ignored my compliment and waved away my hand as I attempted to hand him the prescription. "I couldn't possibly make anything until January."

"I don't want new shoes anyway," Jeney spoke up in an insolent tone that betrayed her distaste for shoes—*any* shoes.

"Take your shoes off," he barked and gestured for me to put her on the table where he was sitting. "Let me see your feet." Lifting her up to sit beside him, I began to undo her laces. She brushed my hands away and pulled the tied shoes off. They dropped to the floor with a thud, and her orthotics fell out.

The shoemaker moved a crumpled piece of brown wrapping paper toward her and smoothed it out. "Here, stand on this," he said gruffly.

Obediently, she stood up and placed her white-socked feet on the paper. Deftly, he ran his fingers around the edge of each foot and with a pencil drew their outline. Wordlessly, he sucked in his breath, looked up at the ceiling, and then at the outline on the paper that remained after Jeney stepped aside. Tears brimmed on his eyelids.

"She's got a serious problem, doesn't she?" he said to me in a much softer voice. Still sitting, he reached up and put his hands around her waist to place her back on the table's edge. With no further comment, he then took each foot in his hands and examined their shape, appearing to memorize them.

"Jeney," he said directly to her, "you and I have something in common."

"What?"

"We have painful feet."

"How did you know that?" she asked with wide blue eyes.

He ignored her question. "You hate shoes too."

"How did you know that?" she repeated.

"Do you see my shoes?" He pointed to the floor. "My feet were like yours when I was a little boy. But they became crippled because there were no helpful shoes or surgery for me. That is why I now make special shoes for special people."

I hoped that the man's personal, rather than clinical,

interest in her would be helpful, but Jeney wasn't impressed. She looked away from his feet to her own.

"Let me see her prescription." He reached out his hand toward the paper I was still holding. "This is correct," he said, and tilted Jeney's face to look into his own. She continued to look down with her eyes and swung her feet in a circular motion. Dangling above the floor, they showed no hint of impediment.

"Let's go pick out some leather for your shoes," he said. Without allowing her to refuse, he slowly stood and lifted her off the table, set her on the floor, took her by the hand, and walked toward a darkened, closetlike room. "What color would you like your shoes to be?" I heard him ask her as they both hobbled away, she still in her sock feet. It was obvious I wasn't to go with them, but I was able to see her almost eagerly choose a piece of red leather.

Still hand-in-hand, they came back to the front of the store while he explained that the shoes would have to be the usual oxford style with laces. It would be six to eight weeks before they could be ready. Even though less defiant, Jeney still didn't say much, but she reached up, took the leather from him, and deliberately put it beside the brown paper with the outline of her feet traced on it.

Red or not, breaking in new orthopedic shoes would be difficult. I was grateful that we would not get them until after the holidays. So when the shoemaker called on December 23 to say he had gotten her shoes done, I was sick, especially when he insisted on seeing her at noon on Christmas Eve day. However, because there was an excited tone in his voice—so different from our first meeting—I couldn't tell him that the shoes would ruin Christmas.

When we told Jeney the shoes were ready, her spirits dropped. Red or not, nothing we said removed the agony of facing another pair of orthopedic shoes, even a promise that she didn't have to begin wearing them until after Christmas Day.

When the day of the appointment arrived, I made excuses not to go. It was difficult to mask my emotion as I watched her daddy help her into her red snowsuit and stocking cap. *If only she could be as bright as the Christmas color she is wearing,* I thought as she trudged out the door.

Over an hour passed. The shop was only a mile from our house. It should have been a fifteen-minute trip. The snow continued to fall, and while I tried to keep busy, I could only sit numbly by a window and watch the mounting whiteness.

"God," I finally begged, "somehow give her a blessing for Christmas. Let her know You care. We try to believe that it was not a mistake when You gave her special feet. But she has such a hard time with the shoes. . . ."

Thumping footsteps on the porch interrupted my prayer. I braced myself with a big smile and started for the door. But before I could get there, Jeney shoved the door open wide, whirling snow to her back. She had a smile that was brighter than her red snowsuit, and she was skipping—almost dancing.

"Mommy! Look! Look!" she squealed.

I couldn't believe my eyes. Shining out from the cuffs of her snowsuit pants were shiny red shoes, designed in a princess style, with a strap and a brass buckle! She danced around the room like a ballerina. Her feet didn't turn over the sides of the shoes. It was easy to see that the shoes were as functional as the usual oxford style, but very comfortable. She had never been able to wear anything like them. It was a miracle! *How had it happened?*

"It was the shoemaker, Mommy!" she said simply,

reading my thought. "He said that God told him how to make them just for me. He made them for me, for church tonight. Look! They're just like other girls wear!"

My husband explained that after the shoemaker had taken impressions of her feet, he had ingeniously fashioned a functional orthopedic shoe with the proper heel and instep and, amazingly, with room for her orthotic insert. This prevented her feet from turning over. Then, with an understanding heart, the shoemaker had designed a princess style.

For Jeney the shoes were the greatest gift she had ever received. She learned through the shoemaker that God cared about her heartache and wanted to ease her suffering. My faith too was strengthened as I agreed that truly God had put it upon the shoemaker's heart to understand her needs.

We remember the red shoes every Christmas, and we've kept them in a box of family treasures. However, with the years came the realization that shoes were not going to correct the problem; surgery ultimately was unavoidable. As she grew older, walking became exhausting and more painful. Running and physical activity were almost an impossibility. We found, too, that surgical methods had changed, and her feet would not be permanently fused. After many years and dozens of pairs of shoes and orthotics, Jeney had two corrective surgeries. Today, she not only wears shoes "like other girls wear," but also has feet "like other girls have."

....

AUTHOR'S NOTE: *According to freelance writer, editor, and teacher Anita Fordyce, "Jeney Ann is today the mother of two sons and walks with straight legs on the path which she believes the Lord is showing her. To our knowledge, the shoemaker is now dead; however, his heartfelt concern and love taught Jeney a valuable lesson and gave her a reason to keep trying. Eventually, a Christian doctor at Temple Sports Medicine in Philadelphia surgically gave her 'new' feet. When he saw her for the first time, he said, 'You've done everything there is to do.' "*

SMALL THINGS

....

Margaret E. Sangster, Jr.

J s anything ever really *small in this life of ours?*
*Or . . . might it be possible that some small
things are, in reality, more significant than* great
things?

*This great truth this virtually unknown Sangster
story brings out, perhaps better than any other story I
have ever known.*

....

*L*ate in the nineteenth century and half into the twentieth, there was no more revered and beloved name in American inspirational literature than Margaret E. Sangster—grandmother, and granddaughter. Time passed, and the name almost slipped into oblivion; but, here and there, there were those who preserved their now tattered stories. Now, at the turn of a new millennium, a new generation of readers is falling in love with these stories all over again. "Small Things," by itself, would be worth bringing the granddaughter [1894–198__] back for.

....

*E*vie was trimming the Christmas tree. She was trimming it with tinsel and glass balls and imitation icicles. She was fastening a chubby small angel on the topmost branch when the doctor came in.

"Hello, darling," she called, peering down at him through a green barricade of branches (for the tree was tall, and Evie was standing on a little red ladder). "Isn't this a swell angel!"

The doctor took off his fur-lined gloves and rubbed

his hands together. He had been driving, and it was very cold, considerably colder than the usual December.

"No," he said, and his voice was as chill as the weather outside. "No, I don't like the angel. It's—it's too fat. It's obese. It looks like a Kewpie."

Evie pouted. "I'm too fat myself," she said. "Christmas—and Christmas candy—has wrecked me, already. Maybe I look a trifle like a Kewpie myself! And yet you like me."

"I'm engaged to you," said the doctor, "so it goes without saying that I like you."

"Usually, it does!" murmured Evie.

"And," the doctor continued, ignoring the interruption, "you're grown up. You're not little. I hate little things."

"I'm not very tall," said Evie. Morosely, she began to clamber down the steps of the red ladder.

"That wasn't what I meant," said the doctor. "You're not tall, no. But you're an adult. That fool angel isn't. It looks like a baby I brought into the world this afternoon. An emergency caesarean, it was. The mother was an Italian—it was her fifth child in five years. A nasty, fat, little wop baby."

Evie was all at once crouched down in front of the

doctor. "Tell me about it," she begged. "Darling, tell me all about it. Just think, born on the afternoon before Christmas. What a break for a baby—"

The doctor snorted. "I'm not an obstetrician," he said. "It isn't my business, seeing that babies are born. On the afternoon before Christmas, or any afternoon. If all the other doctors in the world weren't off at strange places for the holidays, I'd have told them to go to grass, to go somewhere else for their caesarean. But there wasn't any alternative."

Evie's eyes were suddenly round in her little round face. "Don't you like babies, Ned? Or are you only having fun with me? Say you're only having fun! Because it—it isn't nice, this sort of pretend."

"Nice, my hat!" said the doctor. "I was the oldest of nine children. We were poor as mud. I saw my mother falter and fade and die under the burden of nine mouths to feed! Baby mouths—always open; always squalling! I worked for them, to keep them full, those mouths, when I was only a kid myself. Selling papers, printer's devil, running errands, everything. Snatched an education catch as catch can. I'd be a really great surgeon today, Evie, instead of a middling one, if I hadn't wasted so much time on the flock of them."

"Wasted?" queried Evie very softly.

"Wasted!" said the doctor savagely.

There was silence for a moment while snow beat with white insistent fingers against the windowpane. While a fire danced on the hearth. While Evie tried, rather unsuccessfully, to braid her plump, small fingers.

"If we had babies, Ned," she asked softly, "you wouldn't mind it, would you? Keeping their little mouths full, I mean? You wouldn't even mind, would you, if there were nine of them? They couldn't *all* be babies at the same time!"

"There won't be nine of them," said the doctor. Curiously, his eyes watched Evie's fingers, lacing and unlacing. "There won't be any babies, Evie, if I can help it! I've had babies enough in my life. I'm cured . . . I wish—" His tone was petulant; the emergency operation had been a difficult one. "I wish that you'd keep your hands still. I've a headache, and it makes me nervous. . . ."

Evie's fingers were strangely quiet for a moment. So, for that matter, was Evie. And then, with a sudden, swift movement, the fingers were no longer quiet. The fingers of the right hand were very busy removing a ring—a ring that sparkled in the firelight—from one of the fingers of the left hand.

"I'm afraid," said Evie, and it didn't sound like her voice, even to herself, "I'm afraid that I'll make you nervous, Ned, always and always. I'm"—she was dropping the ring into one of the doctor's hands—"I'm sorry."

The doctor hadn't been expecting the ring. It slipped between his fingers and lay on the rug, bright as a tear.

"For crying out loud!" said the doctor. "What are you getting at, Evie? Do you mean that you are—"

"I'm breaking our engagement!" answered Evie.

The doctor should have taken her into his arms and kissed her just then. He should have picked up the ring and forced it back upon the proper one of Evie's fingers. But he wasn't that sort. Instead he said stiffly, "I thought you loved me!"

"I thought I did," answered Evie. She was looking past him. "But I guess I don't. Not as much as I love babies . . . and fat, little angels . . . and other small things. . . ."

The doctor was rising swiftly. How was Evie to know that his head was all one throb and that the tears were very close to his eyes?

"Then it's goodbye?" he asked dully.

"It's goodbye!" agreed Evie.

She turned back to the tree and started, unsteadily, to mount the little red ladder.

The doctor drew on his fur-lined gloves, put on his greatcoat, and reached for his hat. He didn't speak again, neither did he stoop to retrieve the glimmering ring. He only walked out of Evie's living room, and out of Evie's apartment, and out of Evie's life. He only climbed into his waiting car and started, mechanically, to drive downtown through the blurring, blinding snowstorm toward his own apartment. As he went along the great avenue, he passed parks, each with its Christmas tree. They were like Evie's tree, magnified; and church yards, each with its tree, too. Over the door of one church hung a huge electric sign. It said GOOD WILL TOWARD MEN in green and red lights. Seeing it, the doctor muttered something beneath his breath.

It was grim to be the afternoon before Christmas. As the doctor drove along the avenue, he told himself that it was just the sort of a day on which to get unengaged. The snow looked gray instead of white, for it was very close to evening. The arc lights, already blazing, made shallow paths across its grayness. People hurrying to and fro were black, distorted shapes in the general gloom, like gnomes. There wasn't any shine to the eastern sky. There wasn't even the faintest hint of a star.

"I'm dog-tired," the doctor told himself as he drove. "Maybe I'm asleep already and having a nightmare. This isn't happening to me!" (He loved Evie, you see, pretty, plump Evie. Very much indeed!) "It's happening"—he laughed painfully—"to a couple of other fellows."

Indeed, there wasn't any shine in the eastern sky. Even the light from the streetlamps looked dirty. The doctor swung off the avenue and drove through the sedate brownstone-housed street in which he lived. He drew up in front of the old-fashioned, high-stooped place that was his home. It had been converted into apartments, that home. His apartment was on the ground floor.

"Thank God," he said wearily, "that I've no long flights of stairs to climb this night." And then, "I won't even take my car to the garage. It can stand in front until morning, and freeze."

Stiffly, he climbed out of the car. Achingly, he closed the car's door and locked it. And then, fumbling in his pocket for his keys, he mounted the steps of the high stoop. Perhaps it was the snow beating into his face that made him feel so suddenly blind. Perhaps it was something else. Perhaps . . .

The doctor uttered a sharp exclamation and paused. That dark blob on his doormat—he'd thought it was only a shadow, at first. He hadn't known until it cried that it was alive. He'd almost stepped on it! "For the love—" he began.

The blob upon the doormat lifted a furry black blot of a face and uttered a feeble complaint. It did more than lift its face; it lifted an infinitesimal black paw. The doctor saw that the paw was twisted oddly, unnaturally.

"A compound fracture at least," he heard himself saying, then felt foolish when he realized that the black blob was, after all, only a kitten.

A stray kitten, come to his doorstep from some grim, never-never land. A kitten that lifted its tiny, snow-drenched head and sobbed out its baby woe. Sobbed out the agony and fear and lack of understanding that touches the soul of every homeless animal.

The doctor, his arms hanging limply at his sides,

looked down at the forlorn little creature. "I should kick it off the porch," he said savagely. "Hateful, whining little beast." Suddenly all of his own agony and fear and lack of understanding were crystallized in the miserable bit of black fur. "You're the reason for it all!" he shouted down at the kitten. "You and—and things like you! If it weren't for you, I'd still be engaged. I'd—"

Gathering together all of its forces, the kitten struggled to three small feet. It limped piteously across the doormat. It crept agonizingly toward the doctor. It rubbed feebly against his trouser leg.

"Oh, no!" said the doctor. Stooping, he lifted the kitten into the curve of his arm. He held it gingerly, but even so he could tell that it was the thinnest kitten in the whole world! "Oh, goodness!" said the doctor. "Even a kitten's got a right to die indoors on the night before Christmas!"

After all, it *was* nearly dead! And it wasn't a human being, either—it was only an animal. The doctor didn't know much about pets; he'd never had a pet, even when he was a boy. You see, he'd never, really, been a boy. But there was one thing that he did know, even when he was utterly spent, both of body and of soul. He knew surgery. He knew when a leg, even the leg of a worthless kitten, was all out of line. And he knew what should be done to make it assume proper proportions.

"If it were a horse," he said as he unlocked the front door and crossed the general hall to unlock his apartment door, "if it were a horse I'd found on my doorstep"—the idea of a horse on his doorstep didn't seem remotely funny to the doctor at the time—"a horse with a broken leg, I'd call a policeman. And the policeman would come and shoot it and put it out of its misery! But"—the doctor switched on the lights in his living room—"but one can't call a policeman to shoot a kitten."

It was as if the kitten understood. For blinking against the sudden flare of light, the kitten tucked his head into the hollow of the doctor's elbow and tried very feebly to purr.

"He's got guts, anyway," said the doctor. And then, all at once, the doctor reached for his handkerchief. "Oh, Evie!" said the doctor, and blew his nose violently. "Oh, Evie, *my dear . . .*"

The kitten snuggled closer. The purr was more feeble than it had been. Gingerly, the doctor ran his finger along the bone that rose aggressively high on the kitten's spine. "Probably," said the doctor, "he's dying now. But I'll get him some milk, anyway."

He carried the kitten carefully in the direction of his minute kitchenette. "After all, it's bad enough to die, but to die hungry . . ."

Oddly, the doctor found himself wondering whether, years from now, he himself would die hungry. *Heart hungry*.

There was milk in the kitchenette. The maid who came mornings to tidy up had forgotten to put it in the refrigerator, and for once the doctor was grateful for her carelessness. The milk wouldn't be clammy; it wouldn't be necessary to heat it. Still holding the kitten, he poured some of the milk, clumsily, into a cereal dish. Still holding the kitten, he thrust the dish under its nose.

"Drink that!" he commanded harshly. "You little pest!"

The kitten nuzzled its nose down into the saucer of milk. The doctor could feel the quiver of its desperate eagerness. Once, when he was an intern, he had treated a starvation case. He knew the symptoms.

"Slowly, there," he said to the kitten. "Don't go so fast." He held the saucer away for a moment, waiting until the kitten breathed more normally, then held it back again under the quivering nose. After a while the kitten drank more quietly, and under its drying fur the doctor could feel its little sides growing puffy. When finally the saucer was empty, it raised a small face, very daubed with milk. It looked very babyish for a moment. And then with a supreme effort, it lifted its well paw and began weakly to wash the milk from its face.

It was the effort back of that instinctive cleaning that decided the doctor—decided him, for better or for worse.

"A gentleman like you," said the doctor, "deserves two paws to wash with!"

With something like respect in the line of his mouth, in the expression of his eyes, he carried the sated kitten back to the living room. There was a broad mahogany table in the living room that held books and copies of the *A.M.A. Journal* and Evie's picture in a white jade frame. The doctor removed the books and the magazines and put a flat cushion from one of the chairs in their place. But Evie's picture he didn't move.

"Maybe," he said to the picture, "you'd like me better if you could see me do something I'm really good at!"

He laid the kitten on the cushion and went into the bathroom for his emergency kit and some towels. The doctor had his office in a hospital; he hadn't much equipment at home. But he had enough, quite enough, to take care of the needs of a kitten.

Gently carrying his emergency case, he came back to the living room and his patient. The patient was drowsing from the triple result of food, warmth, and pain. With fingers surprisingly tender—for they were very large— he took the kitten's injured paw in his hand and parted the fur. The kitten stirred and whimpered, but he didn't scratch. The kitten seemed to *know*.

"Whew!" said the doctor, surveying the paw. It wasn't only broken, it was mangled. It looked as if it had been chewed. It might have been.

"Amputation," said the doctor.

There was ether in the emergency case. The doctor went into the bathroom again for cotton and a medicine dropper. On the way back he had a thought. *Why not put it to sleep? Permanently. Life's hard enough for whole things, let alone maimed.*

But then he met Evie's pictured eyes, smiling at him from out of their chaste white jade frame. And at almost the same moment he remembered how the kitten had washed its face with one paw.

"I'll show you, honey," he found himself saying wildly to the picture (he'd never called Evie anything like that to her face). "And I won't amputate, either! *It can be done!*"

Little by little, with the aid of the cotton and the medicine dropper, the doctor put the little kitten to sleep. It lay very limp and soft under his hand. Its fur had dried longer than most kitten fur, and fluffier. And then, very tenderly, much more tenderly than he had worked the week before upon the shinbone of a multimillionaire, he began to operate. Upon a thing so tiny that it might have been a smudge of ink, so broken that God, Himself, who watches over sparrows, must have known pity.

It wasn't an easy operation. It took a long while. Once, briefly, the doctor looked up from his task and sighed as he met Evie's watchful gaze. "The patient was on the operating table for a matter of hours," he said. It was the closest the doctor had ever come to being whimsical.

And then, at last, the operation was over, and the sad little paw was miraculously fitted together into some semblance of proper mechanics, held together with splints. (Made of those wooden things that physicians put upon your tongue when they ask you to say, "Ahh.") And over the splints was wound a white, firm, tidy bandage that looked extremely professional. And smelled so, too.

"And that," said the doctor, "is that!"

The kitten stirred, ever so slightly, but it wasn't ready yet to come out of the ether. It had had quite a lot of ether for a kitten. The doctor, seeing it move, looked at his wristwatch. The kitten's movement had been very sleepy.

"My word!" he said, for it was very late, indeed. "*My word!*"

No use now to think about dinner. The restaurant down the street, where he so often ate when he was alone, would be closed. But there was still milk in the kitchenette, and probably bread, too. Bread and milk was good enough for anyone.

But as he was eating the bread and milk out of a deep bowl, the doctor was remembering a telephone conversation he'd had that morning with Evie.

"We'll have our dinner at my place tonight," she had said. "I am, believe it or not, going to cook it. It will be a goose."

The doctor wondered whether Evie was eating her goose alone.

"You can't have your goose and eat it, too!" he found himself saying, and wondered seriously if he had gone mad! Perhaps he had. Perhaps this major operation which he had just performed on such a minor part of life was only one of the delusions that went with madness. Just to make himself feel sane he ate a second bowl of bread and milk, although he didn't really want it. It didn't make him feel sane, either. Just stuffy.

And the kitten wasn't a delusion. For as the doctor left the kitchenette and wended his way toward the living room, he heard sounds of the kitten. Sounds of utter, racking distress.

"How could I have been such a fool!" the doctor questioned as he broke into a trot. "All that ether on top of all that milk! *No wonder!*"

For the kitten was being violently, dreadfully sick at its tummy. It had come out of the ether and had started all over again to taste the bitterness of existence. It raised sad eyes in a peaked black face to the man who had tried so hard to save its life. And then its eyes rolled back strangely and a convulsive shudder took its little body into a dreadful, wrenching paroxysm.

The doctor stood beside the table looking down, dazedly, at the kitten. For a moment he stood there, and then he was galvanized into action. He picked the little thing up swiftly in his clever hands and was forcing open the tiny, rigid mouth.

"Oh, no, you don't!" he said, and his voice was half a sob. "Oh, no, you won't! Not *now*. I won't let you die. Not after bringing you through the hardest operation I've ever done!"

The rigid little mouth was open now. Into it the doctor was dropping a brown liquid. Not much, just a little, from a slim vial in his emergency box. The tremors in the little body began to pass. Two kitten eyes rolled back to normal. And the doctor found that he was wiping beads of sweat from his own forehead.

"You—*kitten!*" he said softly. "Don't you let me catch you acting up again! Don't you dare. . . ." His voice broke on a high note.

But the little kitten. . . . Oh, it wasn't that the little kitten didn't want to mind. Only he'd had rather a bad time of it. Cold, privation, hunger, racking agony, anesthetics. . . . He'd hardly been old enough to know so many sensations, really!

All through the night, the night before Christmas, the doctor fought for a little kitten's life, a life that hung by a black little thread. Fought for that—and for something else. Fought for the rebirth of love in the pictured eyes of a girl. Fought for a rebirth of tenderness. He fought with patient, prayerful hands, and with slim, sharp instruments. He fought with hot compresses and ice packs. He fought, toward dawn, with a stimulant and hot milk. He didn't know that the room was chill with the chill that comes before sunup. He didn't know that it had stopped snowing. He didn't know, even, that it was Christmas Day. He only knew when a tired little kitten thrust out a wee, pinkish tongue to lick his fingers that he had won a victory out of all proportions to the life of a small animal.

"Well," he said as the kitten's rough tongue touched his hand, "you've got eight lives left. As I see it, you should devote 'em all to catching mice—for me."

Wearily, he threw himself down in one of the wide soft chairs that were his greatest luxury. But when the kitten cried softly because it felt abandoned, he got up again. And taking the tiny thing softly into his arms, he went back to the chair.

The kitten snuggled up against his chest, yawning, in a languorous moment of peace after the storm. The doctor yawned, too.

When the maid, who came mornings to tidy up, entered the living room, they were still in the chair, sleeping—a man with a curious pallor on his still face and a mere scrap of a kitten with a front paw in splints and bandages.

The maid, being by this time immune to the oddity of physicians, tiptoed through the living room and toward the kitchen. She made coffee and toast. She pushed the coffeepot to the back of the stove and ate the toast, herself.

It was ten o'clock, perhaps, when she tiptoed through the living room again to answer the buzz of the front door bell. She opened the door with her finger to her lips.

A girl stood there. A pretty, rather plump girl in a fur coat. A girl with trembling lips and dark circles under her eyes.

"I want to see Ned," the girl began. "The doctor," she corrected herself primly.

The maid recognized the girl. She'd dusted the frame around her picture every day for months. But she was a glum maid; she didn't smile.

"The doctor's asleep," she said. "Can I take a message?"

The girl spoke with a rush. "I'm not a patient," she

said. "I am—I was—a friend of the doctor's. He—he dropped something yesterday in my house. I—I found it on the floor after he'd gone. It's something valuable. I wanted to return it to him."

The maid relaxed. She almost achieved a pleasant expression. "You can wait," she said, "I guess." With a jerk of her hand, she indicated a figure in a great chair, a figure seen on a slant through an inner doorway. "He can't sleep *much* longer!"

The girl stepped into the apartment and closed the front door after her. She wasn't a stranger to the place; she'd been there before. She went straight through the inner doorway into the living room—and paused before the miracle of that room. The miracle of a table littered with cotton and bandages and medicine droppers and teaspoons and saucers of clotting milk. And at the calm among the litter—a girl's portrait in a frame of white jade. The miracle of a chair with an exhausted man sprawled in it, a man with a smudge of dust on one cheek, and a slight film of beard (such as most men have before shaving time), and his collar wrenched open at the throat. And threads of lint from torn bandages clinging to his trousers. Of a man sleeping dreamlessly, sleeping with a wee morsel of a black kitten curled up on his chest. *Almost* curled, for one paw was held out stiffly in splints.

The man didn't waken as Evie crossed the room on light, incredulous feet. But the black kitten's eyes came suddenly open. Its pink mouth came open, too, in a yawn. The yawn turned into a tiny yap of pain as the kitten tried to stretch. Stretching wouldn't be easy for quite a few days.

Evie looked at the kitten. She looked at the sleeping man. And then, all at once, her round little face was glorified, and her eyes were as tender as Mary's eyes must have been on the very first Christmas Day of all.

Very quietly, she opened the purse that she carried. It was a frivolous blue purse with a tassel. She took something from it, something that glimmered like the kind of a tear that grows out of extreme happiness. She slipped that something upon the third finger of her left hand.

And then she sat down in a chair, very quietly, to wait.

She was so quiet, in fact, that the small kitten yawned again and went back to sleep.

THE MIRACULOUS STAIRCASE

Arthur Gordon

....

Arthur Gordon

first read this "legend" a number of years ago in The Guideposts Christmas Treasury *and again in Mr. Gordon's wonderful collection of stories,* A Touch of Wonder. *I put the word "legend" in quotes because, unlike most legends, this particular one leaves one with so many unanswered questions.*

When I made my first visit to Santa Fe, at the top of my list of priorities was the Chapel of Our Lady of Light.

I had to see that staircase! *And suddenly,* there it was. *I could only stand there, blinking my eyes in disbelief.*

....

*A*rthur Gordon *(born in 1912), during his long and illustrious career, has edited such renowned journals as* Good Housekeeping, Cosmopolitan, *and* Guideposts. *Along the way, besides penning over two hundred of some of the finest short stories of our time, he also somehow found time to write books such as* Reprisal, Norman Vincent Peale: Minister to Millions, *and* Red Carpet at the White House. *Today, he and his wife Pamela still live on the Georgia coast he has loved since a child.*

....

*O*n that cool December morning in 1878, sunlight lay like an amber rug across the dusty streets and adobe houses of Santa Fe. It glinted on the bright tile roof of the almost completed Chapel of Our Lady of Light and on the nearby windows of the convent school run by the Sisters of Loretto. Inside the convent, the

Mother Superior looked up from her packing as a tap came on her door.

"It's *another* carpenter, Reverend Mother," said Sister Francis Louise, her round face apologetic. "I told him that you're leaving right away, that you haven't time to see him, but he says— "

"I know what he says," Mother Magdalene said, going on resolutely with her packing. "That he's heard about our problem with the new chapel. That he's the best carpenter in all of New Mexico. That he can build us a staircase to the choir loft despite the fact that the brilliant architect in Paris who drew the plans failed to leave any space for one. And despite the fact that five master carpenters have already tried and failed. You're quite right, Sister; I don't have time to listen to that story again."

"But he seems such a nice man," said Sister Francis Louise wistfully, "and he's out there with his burro, and—"

"I'm sure," said Mother Magdalene with a smile, "that he's a charming man, and that his burro is a charming donkey. But there's sickness down at the Santo Domingo pueblo, and it may be cholera. Sister Mary Helen and I are the only ones here who've had cholera.

So we have to go. And you have to stay and run the school. And that's that!" Then she called, "Manuela!"

A young Indian girl of twelve or thirteen, black-haired and smiling, came in quietly on moccasined feet. She was a mute. She could hear and understand, but the Sisters had been unable to teach her to speak. The Mother Superior spoke to her gently. "Take my things down to the wagon, child. I'll be right there." And to Sister Francis Louise: "You'd better tell your carpenter friend to come back in two or three weeks. I'll see him then."

"Two or three weeks! Surely you'll be home for Christmas?"

"If it's the Lord's will, Sister. I hope so." In the street, beyond the waiting wagon, Mother Magdalene could see the carpenter, a bearded man, strongly built and taller than most Mexicans, with dark eyes and a smiling, wind-burned face. Besides him, laden with tools and scraps of lumber, a small gray burro stood patiently. Manuela was stroking its nose, glancing shyly at its owner.

"You'd better explain," said the Mother Superior, "that the child can hear him, but she can't speak."

Goodbyes were quick, the best kind when you leave a place you love. Southwest, then, along the dusty trail, the mountains purple with shadow, the Rio Grande a ribbon of green far off to the right. The pace was slow, but Mother Magdalene and Sister Mary Helen amused themselves by singing songs and telling Christmas stories as the sun marched up and down the sky. And their leathery driver listened and nodded.

Two days of this brought them to Santo Domingo Pueblo, where the sickness was not cholera after all, but measles, almost as deadly in an Indian village. And so they stayed, helping the harassed Father Sebastian, visiting the dark adobe hovels where feverish brown children tossed, and fierce Indian dogs showed their teeth.

At night they were bone-weary, but sometimes Mother Magdalene found time to talk to Father Sebastian about her plans for the dedication of the new chapel. It was to be in April; the Archbishop himself would be there. And it might have been dedicated sooner, were it not for this incredible business of a choir loft with no means of access—unless it were a ladder.

"I told the Bishop," said Mother Magdalene, "that it would be a mistake to have the plans drawn in Paris. If something went wrong, what could we do? But he wanted our chapel in Santa Fe patterned after the Sainte Chapelle in Paris, and who am I to argue with Bishop Lamy? So the talented Monsieur Mouly designs a beautiful choir loft high up under the rose window, and no way to get up to it."

"Perhaps," sighed Father Sebastian, "he had in mind a heavenly choir. The kind with wings."

"It's not funny," said Mother Magdalene a bit sharply. "I've prayed and prayed, but apparently there's no solution at all. There just isn't room on the chapel floor for the supports such a staircase needs."

The days passed, and with each passing day Christmas drew closer. Twice, horsemen on their way from Santa Fe to Albuquerque brought letters from Sister Francis Louise. All was well at the convent, but Mother Magdalene frowned over certain paragraphs. "The children are getting ready for Christmas," Sister Francis Louise wrote in her first letter. "Our little Manuela and the carpenter have become great friends. It's amazing how much he seems to know about us all—"

And what, thought Mother Magdalene, *is the carpenter still doing there?*

The second letter also mentioned the carpenter. "Early every morning he comes with another load of lumber, and every night he goes away. When we ask him by what authority he does these things, he smiles and says nothing. We have tried to pay him for his work, but he will accept no pay—"

Work? What work? Mother Magdalene wrinkled up her nose in exasperation. Had that softhearted Sister Francis Louise given the man permission to putter around in the new chapel? With firm and disapproving hand the Mother Superior wrote a note ordering an end to all such unauthorized activities. She gave it to an Indian pottery maker on his way to Santa Fe.

But that night the first snow fell, so thick and heavy that the Indian turned back. Next day at noon the sun shone again on a world glittering with diamonds. But Mother Magdalene knew that another snowfall might make it impossible for her to be home for Christmas. By now the sickness at Santo Domingo was subsiding. And so that afternoon they began the long ride back.

The snow did come again, making their slow progress even slower. It was late on Christmas Eve, close to midnight, when the tired horses plodded up to the convent door. But lamps still burned. Manuela flew down the steps, Sister Francis Louise close behind her. And chilled and weary though she was, Mother Magdalene sensed instantly an excitement, an electricity in the air that she could not understand. Nor did she understand it when they led her, still in her heavy wraps, down the corridor, into the new, as yet unused chapel where a few candles burned.

"Look, Reverend Mother," breathed Sister Francis Louise. "Look!"

Like a curl of smoke the staircase rose before them, as insubstantial as a dream. Its base was on the chapel floor; its top rested against the choir loft. Nothing else supported it; it seemed to float on air. There were no banisters. Two complete spirals it made, the polished wood gleaming softly in the candlelight.

"Thirty-three steps," whispered Sister Francis Louise. "One for each year in the life of Our Lord."

Mother Magdalene moved forward like a woman in a trance. She put her foot on the first step, then the second, then the third. There was not a tremor. She looked down, bewildered, at Manuela's ecstatic, upturned face. "But it's impossible! There wasn't time!"

"He finished yesterday," the Sister said. "He didn't come today. No one has seen him anywhere in Santa Fe. He's gone."

"But *who* was he? Don't you even know his name?"

The Sister shook her head, but now Manuela pushed forward, nodding emphatically. Her mouth opened; she took a deep, shuddering breath; she made a sound that was like a gasp in the stillness. The nuns stared at her, transfixed. She tried again. This time it was a syllable, followed by another. "José." She clutched the Mother Superior's arm and repeated the first word she had ever spoken. "José!"

Sister Francis Louise crossed herself. Mother Magdalene felt her heart contract. José, the Spanish word for Joseph. Joseph the Carpenter. Joseph the Master Woodworker of—

"José!" Manuela's dark eyes were full of tears. "José!"

Silence, then, in the shadowy chapel. No one moved. Far away across the snow-silvered town Mother Magdalene heard a bell tolling midnight. She came down the stairs and took Manuela's hand. She felt uplifted by a great surge of wonder and gratitude and compassion and love. And she knew what it was. It was the spirit of Christmas. And it was upon them all.

....

AUTHOR'S NOTE: *The wonderful thing about legends is the way they grow. Through the years they can be told and retold and embroidered a bit more each time. This, indeed, is such a retelling. But all good legends contain a grain of truth, and in this case the irrefutable fact at the heart of the legend is the inexplicable staircase itself.*

You may see it yourself in Santa Fe today. It stands just as it stood when the chapel was dedicated almost 123 years ago, except for the banister, which was added later. Tourists stare and marvel. Architects shake their heads and murmur, "Impossible." No one knows the identity of the designer-builder. All the Sisters know is that the problem existed, a stranger came, solved it, and left.

The thirty-three steps make two complete turns without central support. There are no nails in the staircase; only wooden pegs. The curved stringers are put together with exquisite precision; the wood is spliced in seven places on the inside and nine on the outside. The wood is said to be a hard fir variety, nonexistent in New Mexico.

School records show that no payment for the staircase was ever made.

Who is real and who is imaginary in this version of the story? Mother Mary Magdalene was indeed the first Mother Superior. She came to Santa Fe by riverboat and covered wagon in 1852. Bishop J. B. Lamy was indeed her Bishop (best-known to us as the real-life clergyman on which Willa Cather based her literary classic Death Comes to the Archbishop*). And Monsieur Projectus Mouly of Paris was indeed the absent-minded architect.*

Sister Francis Louise? Well, there must have been someone like her. And Manuela, the Indian girl, came out of nowhere to help with the embroidery.

The carpenter himself? Ah, who can say?

CHRISTMAS MAGIC

....

Christine Whiting Parmenter

Jt was the McRitchies' first Christmas for three, and how joyful Mary was that it was to be theirs alone. But she hadn't reckoned on her impulsive husband, on his wrecking her carefully laid plans. Should she cry—or laugh!

This old story is virtually unknown, as has been its authorship. Only after half a century of searching did I discover that it was written by Christine Whiting Parmenter (1877–1953), who wrote prolifically in popu-

lar and inspirational journals early in the twentieth century. More importantly to story aficionados, Parmenter is also the author of "David's Star of Bethlehem," one of the ten most beloved Christmas stories ever written.

....

his Christmas," proclaimed McRitchie proudly, "we shall have a tree!"

He looked into the depths of a frilly basket, to meet the calm gaze of his daughter, six weeks old.

"Yes, old lady," he continued, "it will be *some* tree. And you shall hang up your stocking, and Mother shall hang hers, and even your broken-down old dad may take a chance that Santa will not forget him. You have a wonderful grip upon my finger, daughter. Mary"—with a glance at the baby's mother, who was listening amusedly to his conversation—"isn't this baby unusually husky?"

"Of course!" laughed Mary. Then her eyes grew wistful as she rose and stood beside him. "Mac," she said, "you don't *really* mind because she's not a boy?"

McRitchie looked at her reproachfully. "My dear, this is the fourteenth time you have asked that question, and each time I have replied emphatically that I *prefer* a daughter. I *love* little girls. I like their frills and ruffles. But," McRitchie sighed, "I wish she were twins! I am forty-three years old, Mary; and it takes so long to accumulate a family."

Mary rubbed her cheek against his coat sleeve. "A family of three is not so bad," she replied. "Last year there were only two of us; and we thought that was pretty good—if I remember rightly. But now, Mac, I can hardly wait for Christmas morning! I—I'm glad you want a tree. We'll get a little one and have it on the dining table."

McRitchie turned, looking down on his wife soberly. Then he exploded: "A *little* one! On the *dining* table! Well, I guess not! Mary"—his voice lowered—"I—I never had a Christmas tree. When I was a little kid there was no one who cared enough to fix one for me, not in my memory, you know. All my life I have looked upon them longingly. Maybe I never quite grew up. Anyway—we're going to have a big tree. It must reach within six inches of the ceiling and have all the fixings; miles of tinsel, bushels of popcorn, dozens of lights— everything, just like the pictures you see in magazines. I brought the popcorn home tonight, and all the dinky little electric lights. I—I've just got to have it, Mary."

"Oh, Mac!" said Mary tenderly.

She was continually finding out new things about her husband that made her ache for the lonely little boy he had once been. If she had only known, she would have had a tree for him the year before—the first Christmas after they were married. But this time! Of course, it was absurd to have a great big tree for a baby who would only blink at it; but it was not absurd to have a tree for Mac! It should be the tree of his dreams, to every minutest detail. Mary caught his hand and squeezed it.

"Mac, I'd love it! I've not had a tree for years and years. It'll be a real family Christmas this year—just for the three of us. Oh, Mac! isn't it great to be a family at Christmastime?"

There followed busy and exciting days. As time passed, Mary wondered if her husband spent his entire noon hour in an orgy of shopping at the ten-cent store. Each night he appeared with some new trinkets, which he opened mysteriously and held proudly before Mary's eyes.

These treasures he hid carefully on the top shelf of the china closet, as if he feared the baby might get an untimely glimpse of them. For the first time in his life McRitchie was reveling in the mysteries of Christmas.

But the most important purchases were made the day

Mary went to town. Mrs. Fisher, whose husband worked under McRitchie at the office, and who owed the older man a debt of gratitude, appeared bright and early to care for the baby in Mary's absence. She brought her own baby, a year old and "a perfect darling," cried Mary as the child laughed and held up her little arms.

"I won't be gone long, Mrs. Fisher, and baby will sleep most of the time. If you're hungry there's sponge cake in the box, and we'll have luncheon when I get back."

"Now don't you hurry," said Mrs. Fisher cheerfully. "I love it here. It's a treat to have a change." She glanced about. "Somehow I can't make my house look just like yours," she added wistfully.

Mary smiled. "But you wouldn't want it to look *just* like mine," she answered. "Houses should look like the people who live in them, you know. Your house is lovely, Mrs. Fisher, especially since you got that pretty paper for your living room."

"You didn't mind my getting it like yours?" asked the girl shyly.

"Indeed, no!" cried Mary. "I felt quite flattered. Now, I must go. Just look outside and see the Christmas tree. Mac's going to set it up tonight."

She stopped to drop a kiss on the girl's cheek. It was a cheek that six months before had held a touch of rouge. *It didn't need rouge now*, thought Mary as she walked briskly toward the station. Country air had whipped color into the pale face; and there were other changes. In her mind Mary compared the trim serge dress Mrs. Fisher wore today with the flimsy, transparent shirtwaist she would have worn before, and smiled tenderly at the girl's efforts to copy everything she did herself.

She's a nice little thing, thought Mary. *It was a pity Fisher's sisters considered her beneath their notice. But it was really hardest on the sisters. They had no one but Fisher; and Mrs. Fisher had her husband and the baby, too. A baby was so adorable at Christmas,* thought Mary happily; *and it would be a glorious Christmas this year: a long blissful day with just Mac and the baby. For once, McRitchie hadn't suggested inviting anybody else.*

This last fact Mary hugged jealously to herself. Mac was so dear. He always wanted to share everything he had with everybody who hadn't quite so much, especially the people in the office, whose happiness he considered his special care. But on Christmas it *was* nice to be alone.

One by one Mary had entertained the whole office

force, from Mr. Corey, the mummified head of the firm, to Thomas, the elevator boy. Mary herself had worked in the same office before their marriage, so most of their guests, including Thomas, were old friends. There were new ones now in some of the departments. And Mary's own desk was occupied by Fisher's younger sister. She had recently lost money, and Fisher had asked Mac to take her on, in spite of the coolness between himself and his family, who had never failed to show their disapproval of his marriage. She did her work, Mac said, as if she were conferring a favor upon the firm; but it was work she needed, which was the main thing, he added, with true McRitchie reasoning. It hurt McRitchie a little that Fisher rarely spoke to his sister in the office.

"Not that I really blame him," he said to Mary, "after the snippy way she treats his wife, and taking no notice whatever of the baby."

McRitchie met her at the station, and together they finished the purchases for the tree. Her husband was like a boy, hesitating over each shining ornament as if the fate of a nation rested between a sparkling icicle and a Christmas rose. He ended by purchasing a wonderful Christmas star for the top of the tree, and a red-clothed Santa Claus for the baby.

"Now, don't you dare get anything for me!" she scolded.

"All right," said McRitchie grinning joyfully. "I won't bother about you. Of course, being the whole show myself, it doesn't matter whether anyone remembers you or not. Say, I've got to get back to the office now. Do you think the crowd would notice if I kissed you?"

"Yes, I do," laughed Mary. "Don't you dare!"

McRitchie was rather quiet that night at supper, but his spirits rose during the process of putting the tree up. It *was* a lovely tree, tall and symmetrical as one could wish, reaching, as Mac had stipulated, just six inches from the ceiling.

"I'm dying to trim it, Mary," he said boyishly. "Can't I put a few things on and take 'em off again?"

"No," Mary replied severely. "You must string the popcorn. And why you bought all those cornucopias for candy, when there's no one to eat it but you and me—"

"But—but they always have 'em on Christmas trees in pictures," began McRitchie uneasily. "And—well, it's a pretty big tree for just one little baby, Mary."

"It isn't just for a baby," said Mary gently. "It's for a

little boy who never had a Christmas tree years ago. As for the cornucopias—" She stopped abruptly as a sudden suspicion of truth flashed into her mind. "Mac—it isn't possible—"

The dreadful certainty which was creeping over Mary was confirmed by the guilty look in her husband's face. For a moment she couldn't find her voice, and McRitchie also became strangely dumb. It was the most uncomfortable moment of their married life. Then Mary's sense of humor came to the rescue, and she said shakily: "You might as well confess, Mac. How many people have you invited for Christmas dinner?"

His face brightened suddenly, like sunshine.

"Not one! On my honor, Mary, not one! Do you think I am such a beast as to ask you to get dinner for a crowd, when you haven't half your strength back? But I thought in—in the afternoon, you know—some of 'em might like to see the tree and—and—the baby. We could have some hot chocolate, maybe. I'll make it, Mary, and wash all the dishes. You see, dear, that little Miss Spencer from Vermont is homesick. I caught her crying the other day; and before I thought what I was up to, I asked her to come out Christmas afternoon. I—I think she's had a quarrel with Billy Hall, the bookkeeper. I asked him, too. I thought maybe they'd make up on the train, or something. And then—"

"Yes?" said Mary as he hesitated.

"Well," plunged McRitchie desperately, "there's Miss Knowlton. It's the first Christmas without her mother. She was wild to come. And Mrs. Thompson's just back from the sanitarium and I thought that if—if they dropped in a while it would do her good. The boy would love the tree, Mary, and we could have a package for him. The Taylors can't come because they're going to her mother's; but Thomas almost shot the elevator through the roof, he was so pleased when I asked him. And Mr. Corey—"

"Mr. Corey!" exploded Mary. "You don't mean you asked Mr. Corey, Mac? To our little house—on Christmas?"

"Why not?" answered McRitchie innocently. "I—I'm sorrier for him than for anybody! Living with a tragedy, the way he does. Why, he just ate the invitation right up, Mary. He said Christmas was the hardest day in the whole year."

"Did—did you ask the janitor?" asked Mary weakly.

"Of course," Mac answered soberly, "but he said he

always spent the day with his in-laws." McRitchie's eyes twinkled. "He didn't seem very enthusiastic about in-law Christmases, either. But the Fishers will come, and—oh, look here! are you awfully disappointed, darling? If you only knew—"

"Knew what?" asked Mary, hoping her consternation was absent from her voice.

"How—how awfully lonesome a lonesome Christmas is, dear. Do you know, all those years I lived in a hall bedroom no one ever asked me to a Christmas dinner, or to have a glimpse of a tree, or—or anything. I suppose because I didn't talk about it they thought I had somewhere to go. Once I spent the whole day in the office. It was more like home than any place I knew. Sometimes I wandered around the streets at night, hoping someone would leave a shade up so I could steal a look at all the fun. And now when I have so much, Mary; you and the baby—and a *home*—!"

McRitchie swallowed something as he felt Mary's warm cheek against his own.

"It will be splendid!" she said generously. "I'll ask Mrs. Fisher to help me make some doughnuts. No one will want much supper Christmas night. And there should be a little package for everybody on the tree, jokes—or something to make them laugh. I guess you'll have to do some more shopping, Mac. I can't get to town again to save my life. We'll make a list now and plan everything. We can sing carols, and we'll borrow the Fisher's phonograph and have a Virginia reel. It's lucky we made these two rooms into one. I shan't sleep a wink tonight, I'm so excited."

"Are you?" cried McRitchie happily. "You know, I was sort of afraid you might be disappointed—or something."

If Mary was disappointed she disguised it well, yet there were moments when it vaguely hurt her to think that Mac had asked outsiders on their first Christmas with their baby, well as she understood his impulsive generosity. But these moments were few and far between. This was Mac's first Christmas tree, and she was determined to make it a success. On Christmas Eve, when the last shining bauble was in place, they fairly hugged each other in delight.

"And now," said Mary, "we must be sure we've forgotten no one. Here's the list of names, Mac, and what we've got for them. I couldn't contrive jokes for everyone, but there are enough to make some fun. I haven't forgotten anybody, have I?"

McRitchie took the list, smiling delightedly as he read Mary's jokes. Then suddenly, he exclaimed, "Good land, Mary! I 'most forgot to tell you! I invited Fisher's sisters."

Mary stared. "But—but what shall we do? They hardly speak to Mrs. Fisher, and—"

"I had to, Mary, truly," explained McRitchie. "When I got into the outer hall tonight one of 'em was waiting for me—the one with the long nose."

Mary giggled, and McRitchie added: "You needn't laugh. It's awfully long and pointed. It always seems to get there ahead of her. Well, I saw she wanted to say something, and after a lot of beating about the bush, she lugged out a package done up in ribbons and tissue paper. She asked if I would leave it at her brother's on my way home. It was for the baby."

"Mercy!" gasped Mary in surprise.

"That was what I thought," said McRitchie. "She didn't tell her sister—the one that works in the office, you know. And just then that one burst out of the door and I tucked the package under my coat. Sister had evidently been crying, and Fisher was just behind her. He started when he saw who was talking with me, and nodded like an icicle and went downstairs. He didn't wait for the elevator. I wanted to punch him; but I was sorry for him, too. *He* didn't know about the package. And he loves that little wife of his a good sight more than he did before he married her. But—those girls looked kind of pitiful to me. They're older than Fisher, and they adore him. So—well, I invited them; and they jumped at the chance. I guess they were feeling lonely. Can't you scare up something to give 'em, honey?"

"I may have some new handkerchiefs," said Mary dazedly.

"That'll do for Caroline," said McRitchie, "but I shouldn't want to give anything to Lydia that might draw attention to her nose."

His kindly meaning was so genuine that Mary rocked with mirth.

"A sachet would be almost worse," she laughed. "Well—I've a new crepe tie I'll sacrifice, though I had planned to wear it. Oh, Mac, you are the funniest! I only hope your impulsive invitations won't spoil the party."

"It can't—on *Christmas*," replied McRitchie optimistically. "Come, Mary, let's fill the stockings and go to bed. I'll never forgive myself if you get tired. My dear— I'm afraid your stocking will be pretty empty."

The sparkle in his eyes belied his words, and Mary smiled.

"Don't worry. There won't be much in yours. We'll fill baby's first. Doesn't it look darling, Mac, hanging there between our two big ones?"

McRitchie lifted the tiny pink silk stocking tenderly. "To think, Mary, that such a thing belongs to *us*! It seems incredible. This—won't hold much, honey."

"It'll hold this rubber doll and worsted ball. Somehow, I don't think Miss McRitchie will know the difference."

"And I've got two little candy canes. We'll put those in for looks. There, Mary! Who dares tell me that dreams don't come true."

"Not I," said Mary as McRitchie kissed her.

"Now shall I fill your stocking while you turn your back, or—"

"You'll fill it while I fix the furnace, and then you'll scoot upstairs. This is a new job to me. I want the whole place to myself. Do you know, Mary, I feel just like a kid."

"You won't peek at things when I'm gone then?" asked Mary sternly.

"Cross my heart," laughed Mac as he descended cellarward.

It was a glorious Christmas morning. A snowstorm the night before had frosted everything. Miss McRitchie awoke her parents with a demand for breakfast, and then seconds later her dad was wishing her a Merry Christmas.

Afterward (Mac hadn't even allowed Mary to start the coffee), they sat on the floor before the fireplace, and baby cuddled in her father's arms.

"Don't try to tell me this kid's too young to enjoy Christmas!" exclaimed McRitchie. "She's trying to eat up all her presents."

"If you let her eat those candy canes you may regret it," replied the baby's mother. "Open your stocking, Mac, I can't wait another moment to look at mine. There's only one thing in yours, except the oranges to make it bulky, so don't be disappointed."

"And there's *nothing* in yours except the bulky thing. Your present's in that box beside the fender. . . . Oh, Mary! The idea of your getting me those fur-lined gloves! Is it possible my thrifty wife is turning out a spendthrift! I love 'em, dear. Come nearer so I can hug you."

"Wait!" said Mary. She was untying her box as excitedly as a child. "Oh, Mac! Mac!" Her eyes swam with tears as she buried her face in the soft furs—furs she had wanted for so long. "Don't you talk about extravagance," she said shakily. "I know now why you wouldn't get an overcoat. And your old one's so—*so shabby*—"

"It is *not*. And even if it were, think how the other men will envy me my stunning wife. Put 'em on, dear—quick! Are they what you want? You can change them if—"

"Change them!" echoed Mary indignantly. "Mac, I feel like a duchess. I shall want to wear them every minute! I shall go to *bed* in them! Oh, Mac!"

....

The first of the McRitchie guests to arrive were the Fishers, at three o'clock, armed with a baby, a blossoming azalea plant for Mary, and what McRitchie called a "monument of doughnuts," since Mrs. Fisher had insisted on making every one. Mary had made sugar cookies and gingerbread; a huge caldron of chocolate was on the stove, and there was grape juice and lemonade for those who wanted to cool off. Mary, seeing the Fishers turn in at the gate, hoped devoutly that Fisher's sisters would be the last arrivals. In a crowd things would be less awkward.

"Merry Christmas!" welcomed McRitchie, throwing wide the door. "Fisher, you dump those doughnuts in the kitchen. Mary's upstairs, Mrs. Fisher. I believe she wants you. She's going to rope you into pouring chocolate when the guests arrive."

This had been an inspiration on Mary's part. She was going to show those haughty sisters that Mrs. Fisher could do things gracefully. She had telephoned that morning to ask as a favor that Mrs. Fisher wear her dark blue taffeta. It was her most becoming dress, and Mary was bound she look her best.

"Come up!" she called over the banister. "Baby's asleep. I hope she'll sleep an hour longer, for Mac's sure to keep her up outrageously. I know her habits will be in ruins by night; but we can't help it. Christmas comes but once a year and—oh, Mrs. Fisher, how sweet your baby looks in that little jacket! And her hair is curling! I told you it would curl. Oh, I wish the Taylors were coming with all their children! This is an awfully grown-up Christmas party; just your baby and ours, and little Harold Thompson. Thomas is only fourteen, but I suppose he'd resent being called a child."

"Mr. Fisher's sister Lydia made the little jacket," said Mrs. Fisher proudly, "and Caroline sent that cunning pin. She gave it to Mr. Fisher in the office. I thought I'd let her wear them both. It—it made Mr. Fisher so happy to have them do it."

"Of course it did!" said Mary gently. "Here—let me carry the baby down for you. I can't keep away from her, she looks so dear."

Inwardly Mary was exulting. Fisher's sisters could *not* resist that baby! For the first time she felt glad of Mac's impulsive invitation.

"Merry Christmas, Mrs. McRitchie!" cried Fisher joyously. "Say, that's some tree! And look, honey!"—turning to his wife—"at that little stocking. Mac left it up for the crowd to see."

Mary smiled. "It broke his heart to take it down this morning, so I told him to leave it there, though it looks rather limp without the dolly. Open the door, Mac, here comes Miss Knowlton and the Thompsons; and—yes, there's Mr. Corey's car! He's got Thomas with him and Miss Spencer and Billy Hall. He must have picked them up on the way. And—why, Mac! There *are* the Taylors! Every one of them! Isn't that too good to be true? And—and—"

Mary did not mention the last two figures turning in at the gate. She was dimly conscious that Mrs. Fisher had darted toward the kitchen with her baby; but amid all the confusion she saw with joy that Fisher went forward and kissed both his sisters, and she knew suddenly that everything would be all right.

"I don't know what you'll think of us," Mrs. Taylor was explaining breathlessly, "to say we weren't coming, and then to *come*! But Mother was really too sick to have us; just a grippy cold, but she was afraid we'd all get it. So after dinner George said to come along, he knew the McRitchies wouldn't care. We tried to telephone but the wires were down. The children were crazy to see the baby, and—"

"Oh, I'm so glad!" said Mary. "The one thing this party lacked was children. Merry Christmas, Thomas! You know where to find the gingerbread. Hello, Miss Knowlton! I'll kiss you when I get near enough. Merry Christmas, Miss Spencer! You don't know how glad we are to see you! And this is Billy Hall, of course. You see, I have heard about you, even if we've never met. And you two are Mr. Fisher's sisters. It's splendid that you could come. Mr. Fisher, will you find your wife and ask her to look after things while I show these people where to leave their wraps? Merry Christmas, Mr. Corey! Can you steer a double-runner? Those who want to coast may keep their things on, then the rest of you may come upstairs."

Two hours later, when the coasting party was over and the whole crowd had made the acquaintance of Miss McRitchie, Mac turned on the lights and proudly displayed the tree.

"There's not a thing on it for any of you Taylors," mourned Mary, "but there's popcorn galore, and candy—"

"Don't you worry," said Mrs. Taylor cheerfully. "The children have had one tree already, and Junior doesn't want anything but the three bright pennies that were in his stocking. He's been hanging on to them all day. I believe he thinks they're *gold*. As for George and me—"

"Mary," interrupted Mac, "where's some tissue paper? I've a present for Taylor and nothing to do it up in."

"You see!" laughed Mrs. Taylor. "Junior!"—with a dash for her youngest—"don't tear the popcorn off the tree. It's for decoration."

"No, it isn't," contradicted McRitchie. "You can have a whole string in a minute, Sonny. Thanks, Mary. Is everybody here? We might as well distribute these costly gifts."

"Present," called Fisher from the corner. "Fire ahead, Mac."

Yes, everyone was there, thought Mary as she looked around on the group. In Mac's big chair was Lydia Fisher, the Fisher baby on her lap. Fisher, himself, was sitting between his wife and his younger sister, brazenly holding a hand of each, and looking, somehow, more manly than of old. Mac had been right when he urged Fisher to buy a place in the country and settle down. Responsibility, and perhaps the trouble he'd been through, were obliterating the weak lines about his mouth. Billy Hall stood where he could just look down upon Miss Spencer's smooth brown hair, without appearing to; and Mr. Corey was holding Mary's baby with all the ease of a veteran grandfather. The three Thompsons sat very close together on the davenport, as if they could bear no further separation after the year Mrs. Thompson had spent in a sanitarium. Miss Knowlton's plain, good-natured face was wreathed in smiles, and Thomas-of-the-elevator was fairly beaming. *It was a happy crowd*, thought Mary, as she sat down on the floor among the four young Taylors.

The fun began when McRitchie presented Taylor with a pencil attached to a phenomenally long string. This brought laughter, because Taylor was always losing his pencil in the office, and borrowing one. Thomas blushed with pleasure and embarrassment at the gift of a safety razor, while Fisher immediately offered to show him how to use it. Miss Knowlton received a cake of scented soap, because she was constantly regretting the lack of that article in the office coatroom. And Mr. Corey, who was an inveterate smoker, but who always advised everybody else to leave the weed alone, was presented with a box of chocolate cigars, marked WARRANTED HARMLESS.

But it was Fisher, who, after the gifts were all distributed, brought down the house by presenting McRitchie with a beribboned package which proved to be a copy of *How to be Happy Though Married*. Everyone shouted, and there was renewed rejoicing when Mac declared he didn't need it, and passed it on to Billy Hall, which for some obscure reason brought the color to Miss Spencer's face.

Afterward, Mrs. Fisher presided at the chocolate pot, and everybody squeezed into the dining room; that is, everyone but Mr. Corey. Miss McRitchie had dropped asleep in Mr. Corey's arms, so he refused to move; and Mary, seeing that her baby was filling a long-felt want, didn't insist. Later, Jerry Thompson, who could really sing, started some carols that everybody knew, and they all joined in. But the crowning fun of the day was the Virginia reel. None knew that it was a whispered word from Mary that caused Mr. Corey to invite Mrs. Fisher to head the reel with him. Mary herself was at the other end with Thomas, whose past life had not included dancing, but whose Irish feet and wit were to cause him no uneasiness.

It was a glorious reel. Everyone danced but Fisher's sister, Lydia, who refused to lay down her precious burden to join the fun. Then came a stampede for lemonade; and when every tumbler and teacup in the house was filled, it was Mr. Corey who raised his glass (it was a jelly tumbler!) and cried: "Here's to the McRitchies—God bless 'em." The cheer that followed threatened to wake the sleeping babies.

....

They were alone at last—the McRitchies. They stood looking down upon their daughter, slumbering sweetly in a corner of the davenport, unmindful that her first party was just over.

"It was a wonderful Christmas tree, daughter," said

McRitchie, "and I was proud of you. I only hope that Mother is not all worn out."

"I'm not," said Mary. "And even if I were, Mac, I shouldn't care, after seeing Mrs. Fisher's face when Fisher told her that his sisters would spend the night in her little guest room. *That* wouldn't have happened if we had not had the party."

"And when I opened the door, Mary, and discovered Billy Hall with his arms around the little Spencer girl—"

"You did?" cried Mary.

"I tried to vanish gracefully, but it was too late. Miss Spencer was the color of the red, red rose, my dear, but Billy was very bold. He said, 'Close the door, please.'"

"That's lovely," said Mary. "Mac, dear, we must go up to bed. Take down the baby's stocking and—why, look! There's something in it! It's stuffed full!"

"And heavy!" exclaimed McRitchie, lifting it wonderingly. "And here's a card. Come here on my knee, Mary, and see what's up. That's Mr. Corey's writing. It says"—McRitchie caught his breath—"it says, 'A nest egg for little Miss McRitchie, from the derelicts and others to whom her parents have given a happy Christmas.'"

Mac looked speechlessly at Mary as he emptied the little stocking into her lap. Quarters, dimes, gold pieces, three bank notes, even Junior Taylor's precious Christmas pennies were among the hoard. The McRitchies were still unable to speak. Then Mac unwrapped a scrap of paper, revealing another gold piece and a penciled scrawl.

"Mr. McRitchie, I want to give this to your baby. It's the best I have. Mr. Corey gave it to me today, but I haven't any use for it, truly. I never had a family, and no one ever asked me anywhere but you. I didn't know there was such things as Christmases like this. Yours truly, Thomas."

"Oh, dear!" said Mary, chokingly. "Oh, *dear!*"

"For five cents," said McRitchie, huskily, "I could weep. This is a real nest egg, Mary. We'll add to it every year, and when that sleepyhead is ready to go to college—"

McRitchie stopped abruptly, and became absorbed in the treasure on Mary's lap.

"Mr. Corey must have given the gold pieces," he said slowly; "but whoever gave those bank notes couldn't afford it. I bet one was from Miss Knowlton—but—we'll never know. Maybe that's the beauty of it, dear. And that poor kid, Thomas—"

McRitchie's glasses suddenly needed wiping, and there came a silence before Mary spoke.

"Well, dear," she said, "I think it is up to us to see that Thomas makes something of his life. He shan't spend all of his days taking people from the first floor to the tenth of the Corey Building. We'll manage somehow to give that boy a chance.

"Oh, Mac, what a dear world it is! So full of lovely opportunities to lend a hand! When I look at that little stocking and think what it meant to some of them to be so generous, I'm just ashamed. I—I wish I were more like you, Mac. I've been so selfish. I wanted dreadfully to have the day alone with you and the baby. And now—"

"You dear goose!" cried McRitchie tenderly. "Don't you know that's what I wanted, too?"

And those words were all that Mary needed to make her Christmas the perfect day.

THE MAN WHO
MISSED CHRISTMAS

....

J. Edgar Parks

![drop cap G] **G**eorge Mason was a successful business executive who had little use for Christmas. He was an island unto himself. Then something totally unexpected occurred. Something horrifying. And then . . . total darkness.

Over the years, so many people have urged me to include this story that it has gradually risen through the file system to the top.

Its day has come.

n Christmas Eve, as usual, George Mason was the last to leave the office. He stood for a moment at the window, watching the hurrying crowds below, the strings of colored Christmas lights, the fat Santa Clauses on the street corners. He was a slender man in his late thirties, this George Mason, not conspicuously successful or brilliant, but a good executive. He ran his office efficiently and well.

Abruptly, he turned and walked over to a massive safe set into the far wall. He spun the dials and swung the heavy door open. A light went on, revealing a vault of polished steel as large as a small room. George Mason carefully propped a chair against the open door of the safe and stepped inside. He took three steps forward, tilting his head so that he could see the square of white cardboard taped just above the top row of strongboxes. On the card a few words were written. George Mason stared at those words, remembering. Exactly one year ago he had entered this self-same vault. . . .

He had planned a rather expensive, if solitary, evening. He had decided he might need a little additional cash. He had not bothered to prop the door; ordinarily, friction held the balanced mass of steel in place. But only that morning the people who serviced the safe had cleaned and oiled it. And then, behind George Mason's back, slowly, noiselessly, the ponderous door swung shut. There was a click of spring locks. The automatic light went out, and he was trapped, entombed in the sudden and terrifying dark.

Instantly, panic seized him. He hurled himself at the unyielding door. He gave a hoarse cry, the sound was like an explosion in that confined place. In the silence that followed he heard the frantic thudding of his heart. Through his mind flashed all the stories he had heard of men found suffocated in time vaults. No time clock controlled this mechanism; the safe would remain locked until it was opened from the outside. Tomorrow morning.

Then the realization struck him. No one would come tomorrow—tomorrow was Christmas Day. Once more he flung himself at the door, shouting wildly, beating with his hands until he sank on his knees, exhausted. Silence again, high-pitched, singing silence that seemed deafening.

George Mason was no smoker; he did not carry matches. Except for the tiny luminous dial of his watch, the darkness was absolute. The blackness almost had texture. It was tangible, stifling. The time now was 6:15. More than thirty-six hours would pass before anyone entered the office. Thirty-six hours in a steel box three feet wide, eight feet long, seven feet high. Would the oxygen last?

Like a flash of lightning a memory came to him, dimmed by the passage of time. What had they told him when they installed the safe? Something about a safety measure for just such a crisis as this. . . . Breathing heavily, he felt his way around the floor. The palms of his hands were sweating. But in the far right-hand corner, just above the floor, he found it—a small, circular opening some two inches in diameter. He thrust his finger into it and felt, faint but unmistakable, a cool current of air.

The tension release was so sudden that he burst into tears. At last, he sat up. Surely he would not have to stay trapped for the full thirty-six hours. Somebody would miss him, would make inquiries, would come to release him.

But who? He was unmarried and lived alone. The

maid who cleaned his apartment was just a servant; he had always treated her as such. He had been invited to spend Christmas Eve with his brother's family, but children got on his nerves and expected presents.

A friend had asked him to go to a home for elderly people on Christmas Day and play the piano (George Mason was a good musician). But he had made some excuse or other; he had intended to sit at home, listening to some new recordings he was giving himself for Christmas.

George Mason dug his nails into the palms of his hands until the pain balanced the misery in his mind. He had thrown away his chances of being found. Nobody would come and let him out. Nobody, nobody.

Marked by the luminous hands of the watch, the leaden-footed seconds ticked away. He slept a little, but not much. He felt no hunger, but he was tormented by thirst. Miserably, the whole of Christmas Day went by, and the succeeding night.

On the morning after Christmas the head clerk came into the office at the usual time. He opened the safe, but did not bother to swing the heavy door wide, then went into his private office.

No one saw George Mason stagger out into the corridor, run to the water cooler, and drink great gulps of water. No one paid any attention to him as he descended to the street and took a taxi home. There he shaved, changed his wrinkled clothes, ate some breakfast, and returned to his office, where his employees greeted him pleasantly but casually.

On his way to lunch that day he met several acquaintances, but not a single one had noticed his Christmas absence. He even met his own brother, who was a member of the same luncheon club, but his brother failed to ask if he had enjoyed Christmas.

Grimly, inexorably, the truth closed in on George Mason. He had vanished from human society during the great festival of brotherhood, and no one had missed him at all. Reluctantly, almost with a sense of dread, George Mason began to think about the true meaning of Christmas. Was it possible that he had been blind all these years with selfishness, indifference, with pride? Wasn't Christmas the time when men went out of their way to share with one another? Wasn't giving, after all, the essence of Christmas?

All through the year that followed, with little hesitant deeds of kindness, with small, unnoticed acts of unselfishness, George Mason tried to prepare himself. Now, once more, it was Christmas Eve. Slowly, he backed out of the safe, closed it. He touched its grim steel face lightly, almost affectionately, as if it were an old friend. He picked up his hat and coat, and certain bundles. Then he left the office, descended to the busy street.

There he goes now in his black overcoat and hat, the same George Mason as a year ago. Or is it? He walks a few blocks, then flags a taxi, anxious not to be late. His nephews are expecting him to help them trim the tree. Afterward, he is taking his brother and sister-in-law to a Christmas play. Why is he so happy? Why does this jostling against others, laden as he is with bundles, exhilarate and delight him?

Perhaps the card has something to do with it, the card he taped inside his office safe last New Year's Day. On the card is written, in George Mason's own hand: *To love people, to be indispensable somewhere, that is the purpose of life. That is the secret of happiness.*

GRR-FACE

....

Gary B. Swanson

e all take our senses for granted, placing, instead, undue value on monetary things. We'd be
*happy, we say, if Publisher's Clearing House made us
multimillionaires. But multimillionaires are rarely very
happy, so there must be something wrong with that asser-
tion. This little story reminds us that there are some
things that dwarf mere money.*

*Gary Swanson, of Columbia, Maryland, has taught
both on the high school and college levels, has been in public*

relations, has edited such publications as Listen Magazine, Collegiate Quarterly, *and* Cornerstone Connections, *and has written about a thousand poems, essays, and short stories. This particular story is true, and took place in central California a number of years ago.*

....

The mother sat on the simulated-leather chair in the doctor's office, picking nervously at her fingernail. Wrinkles of worry lined her forehead as she watched five-year-old Kenny sitting on the rug before her.

He was small for his age and a little too thin, she thought. His fine blond hair hung down smooth and straight to the top of his ears. But white gauze bandages encircled his head, covering his eyes and pinning his ears back.

In his lap he bounced a beaten-up teddy bear. It was the pride of his life, yet one arm was gone and one eye missing. Twice his mother had tried to throw it away, to replace it with a new one, but he had fussed so much she had relented. She tipped her head slightly to the side and smiled at him. *It's really about all he has,* she sighed to herself.

A nurse appeared in the doorway. "Kenny Ellis," she announced, and the young mother scooped the boy up and followed the nurse toward the examination room. The hallway smelled of rubbing alcohol and bandages. Children's crayon drawings lined the walls.

"The doctor will be with you in a moment," the nurse said with an efficient smile. "Please be seated."

The mother placed Kenny on the examination table. "Be careful, honey, not to fall off."

"Am I up very high, Mother?"

"No, dear, but be careful."

Kenny hugged his teddy bear tighter. "Then I don't want Grr-Face to fall either."

The mother smiled. The smile twisted at the corners into a frown of concern. She brushed the hair out of the boy's face and caressed his cheek, soft as thistledown, with the back of her hand. As the office music drifted into a haunting version of "Silent Night," she remembered the accident for the thousandth time.

She had been cooking things on the back burners for years. But there it was, positioned out in front, the water almost boiling for oatmeal.

The phone rang in the living room. It was another one of those "free offers" that cost so much. At the very moment she returned the phone to the table, Kenny screamed in the kitchen: the galvanizing cry of pain that frosts a mother's veins.

She winced again at the memory of it and brushed aside a warm tear slipping down her cheek. Six weeks they had waited for this day to come. "We'll be able to take the bandages off the week before Christmas," the doctor had said.

The door to the examination room swept open, and Dr. Harris came in. "Good morning, Mrs. Ellis," he said brightly. "How are you today?"

"Fine, thank you," she said. But she was too apprehensive for small talk.

Dr. Harris bent over the sink and washed his hands carefully. He was cautious with his patients but careless about himself. He could seldom find time to get a haircut, and his straight black hair hung a little long over his collar. His loosened tie allowed his collar to be open at the throat.

"Now, then," he said, sitting down on a stool, "let's have a look."

Gently he snipped at the bandage with scissors and unwound it from Kenny's head. The bandage fell away, leaving two flat squares of gauze taped directly over Kenny's eyes. Dr. Harris lifted the edges of the tape slowly, trying not to hurt the boy's tender skin.

Kenny slowly opened his eyes and blinked several times as if the sudden light hurt. Then he looked at his mother and grinned. "Hi, Mom," he said.

Choking and speechless, the mother threw her arms around Kenny's neck. For several minutes she could say nothing as she hugged the boy and wept in thankfulness. Finally, she looked at Dr. Harris with tear-filled eyes. "I don't know how we'll ever be able to pay you," she said. "Since my husband died, it's been hard for us."

"We've been over all that before," the doctor interrupted with a wave of his hand. "I know how things are for you and Kenny. I'm glad I could help."

The mother dabbed at her eyes with a well-used handkerchief, stood up, and took Kenny's hand. But just as she turned toward the door Kenny pulled away and stood for a long moment looking uncertainly at the doctor. Then he held his teddy bear up by its one arm to the doctor.

"Here," he said, "take my Grr-Face. He ought to be worth a lot of money."

Dr. Harris quietly took the broken bear in his two hands. "Thank you, Kenny. This will more than pay for my services."

....

he last few days before Christmas were especially good for Kenny and his mother. They sat together in the long evenings, watching the Christmas tree lights twinkle on and off. Bandages had covered Kenny's eyes for six weeks, so he seemed reluctant to close them in sleep at night. The fire dancing in the fireplace, the snowflakes sticking to his bedroom window, the two small packages under the tree—all the lights and colors of the holiday fascinated him.

And then, on Christmas Eve, Kenny's mother answered the doorbell. No one was there, but a large box was on the porch, wrapped in metallic green paper with a broad red ribbon and bow. A tag attached to the bow identified the box as intended for Kenny Ellis.

With a grin, Kenny tore the ribbon off the box, lifted the lid, and pulled out a teddy bear—his beloved Grr-Face. Only it now had a new arm of brown corduroy and two new button eyes that glittered in the soft Christmas light. Kenny didn't seem to mind that the new arm didn't match the other one. He just hugged his teddy bear and laughed.

Among the tissue in the box, the mother found a card. "Dear Kenny," it read, "I can sometimes help put boys and girls back together, but Mrs. Harris had to help me repair Grr-Face. She's a better bear doctor than I am. Merry Christmas! Dr. Harris."

"Look, Mother," Kenny smiled, pointing to the button eyes. "Grr-Face can see again—just like me!"

JOE WHEELER, Ph.D., Emeritus Professor of English at Columbia Union College in Maryland, compiled the four volumes in the *Christmas in My Heart*© series. He is Senior Fellow for Cultural Studies at the Center for the New West in Denver. He has established nine libraries in schools and colleges as well as working on his own collection (as large as some college libraries). Joe and his wife Connie are the parents of two grown children, Greg and Michelle, and now make their home in Conifer, Colorado.